Frightliner

And Other Tales of the Supernatural

Colleen Drippé
and Karina Fabian

Laser Cow Press

ROCKLEDGE, FL

Laser Cow Press
ROCKLEDGE, FL

Publisher's Note: This is a work of fiction. Names, characters, places, and incidents are a product of the author's imagination. Locales and public names are sometimes used for atmospheric purposes. Any resemblance to actual people, living or dead, or to businesses, companies, events, institutions, or locales is completely coincidental.

Book Layout © 2017 BookDesignTemplates.com
Cover art by Sean Lowery

Frightliner and Other Tales of the Supernatural/Colleen Drippé and Karina Fabian. — 1st ed.
ISBN 978-1-7334471-6-4

To all those wonderful horror writers who enriched our childhoods. (heh heh) —Colleen

To all the wonderful horror writers whose work freaked me out even years after I closed the book. (whimper) —Karina

Contents

Frightliner

The Friday night Reba walked out on Daniel, there wasn't a cloud in the sky. The stars were scattered about like fat, yellow jewels, fighting with the nearly full moon for dominance over the blackness. It was the new pickup that did it. She'd worked overtime at the hospital—weeks and weeks of it—to make the down payment on a new trailer. And then he'd gone out and bought a new Chevy pickup! It was the last straw.

"I didn't sign on that thing," she told him as she packed. "You can pay for it yourself."

"No problem, Babe," he answered right back. But she knew he was bluffing. He didn't really think she'd stay away for good. They'd only been married two years and mostly they still liked each other pretty much.

And, she told herself, as she drove off in her beat-up Honda, he was probably right. She might come back. But not right off.

She stopped at a diner and called her sister in El Paso. Told Melanie she was on her way, invited herself for the weekend. She didn't want to give up her job as an aide. Not for Daniel's sake.

It was some drive from Roswell, where she had lived these past two years, and she was too mad to check the gas tank. She was thinking about her things she had packed—more than one weekend's worth—and what Daniel was doing right now—probably drinking and driving around in the new pickup. Maybe he'd get a DUI. She thought about that, smiling a fierce little smile.

About six miles from Carlsbad, she ran out of gas.

She said a word her mother wouldn't have liked and coasted the car to the side of the road. She checked her cell phone, found it dead, too. And Daniel had taken the charger. She said a few more words. She'd have to wait for a cop or something, she guessed, and reached back to make sure all the doors were locked.

But no cop came. The moon shone steady and without concern, and, no doubt, the constellations moved on their busy way across the sky, but only a couple cars went by and nobody stopped. She wasn't sure she wanted them to.

She was just resolving to get another car charger for her cell phone as soon as she got to her sister's when a semi pulled up behind her. Weird. She hadn't seen the lights in her mirror, hadn't heard a thing. But it had lights. She saw them for a moment before they were turned off.

Her father had been a truck driver, and she had no illusions about knights of the road stuff. He had beat her mom, cussed at the neighbors, and finally jackknifed a semi in the middle of

Atlanta, killing himself and doing in a load of chickens along with a sports car and part of a street sign.

Still, maybe this guy would be okay. After all, he worked for a company, and he would want to keep his job. He wouldn't try anything funny—or if he did, it would be the sort of funny stuff she could handle. In fact, she thought, maybe a bit of funny stuff was just what she needed. She waited for her rescuer to get out of the truck.

But nothing happened. The semi sat there, seemingly parked for the night, lights off, black against the radiant sky, like a big rectangle cut out of the world.

She grew more and more impatient. If only someone else would drive along! But no one did, and she was growing downright chilly in her shorts and belly shirt. It'd been hot earlier that day and she'd been—well, that didn't much matter now. At least Daniel'd gotten a hint of what he'd be missing out on. Tentatively, she opened her door, wincing as the dome light came on. Surely the driver could see it from the truck. He would know that someone was in the car.

Of course, that was why he had not come out to check on her, she thought with a surge of relief. He probably thought it was an abandoned car. But now...

She stepped out onto the gravel, hearing for the first time how loud the crickets sang. She smelled the strong scent of the cooling air. Too early for snow. Too warm, still anyway, though she cursed herself for not thinking to put on jeans before making her big exit. She peered at the cab, but nothing moved.

"Hello!" she called, moving closer. She could not make out a logo on the truck. It was dark, dark paint. She had an impression that the shape was—not wrong exactly, but not usual. It was an older model, she decided. An old truck.

She had reached the door.

"Anyone there?" she called, hesitating to step up and look inside. What if something had happened to the driver? What if he were dead? What if she opened the door and a body spilled out onto the road?

But that was silly. He had just pulled up. Probably he was rummaging around in his berth for some tools.

But what if he was dead? What if she took hold of the door and—and what if he was right there, watching her?

She had almost decided to go back to her own car. But the thought of the semi parked behind her, silently cutting its chunk from the sky, was in some strange way even more frightening than opening the door. She reached up for the handle and pulled herself up level with the window.

The handle turned in her hand.

It was then she knew she had done the wrong thing. If only someone else had come—she prayed for someone else. A cop. Even a car full of good-old boys. Anyone.

The crickets fairly screamed their shrill and mindless song; the scent of the Russian knapweed was overpowering. But it wasn't strong enough to hide another smell, a dark earthy smell. A smell of death mellowed by long usage.

The door opened.

Reba froze, clutching the handle, balancing there with the driver's seat in front of her. She tried to speak, to call, but nothing would come out. She hung there, thinking of death, while the night passed, and the stars moved, and the moon looked in over her shoulder. Finally, she climbed into the truck.

"Daniel," she whimpered. She was ready to forgive the new pickup, but it was too late. Something moved in the back, and she turned in the driver's seat and saw a pale face, caught in the moonlight, eyes gleaming. She had an impression of lank hair, grizzled beard. And then two hands reached up to take her shoulders and she saw the mouth open.

She screamed at last, drowning the noise of the crickets, drowning the beating of her heart, the wrenching sounds of her own dislocating joints as something drank its fill, savaging its prey, ripping—

When she knew she was dying, she ceased to scream. For one awful moment, she looked into eternity and then, remembering some scraps of childhood religion, she tried to pray.

With a final snarling rip, the thing tore out her throat and cast her body out onto the road.

***

Jay Carlson's head bobbed back and forth, and he tapped the wheel of his 2013 Kenworth

W900L as he cruised south on NM Highway 285. He was singing to some upbeat country song he didn't know the words to, just making them up as he went along. Nothing was going to break his mood.

He'd been lucky this run—light traffic, no holdups—so he'd treated himself to a detour to Roswell, staying overnight there and checking out the museum before heading on his way. He was glad he did. The gift shop had been almost as much fun as the museum, he thought, as he grinned at the acrobatic alien perched on his dashboard, swaying with the bumps in the road.

Suddenly, a loud blaring, like a tortured water buffalo, followed by a *whoosh!* that shook even his fully loaded rig, jarred him out of his happy daydream.

"Jerk!" he yelled at the taillights of the aged 18-wheeler that had just passed him. "What's your hurry?"

For a moment, he considered increasing his own speed; any Smokeys in the area would no doubt get old leadfoot first, giving him time to slow to legal speed, but he decided against it. Sometimes, troopers here worked in pairs, and the chance of a delay and a ticket wasn't worth the time he might save. Besides, he wasn't sure he wanted to catch up with the truck. For some reason, the thought of seeing it again made him shudder.

He didn't have much time to dwell on it. Here came more trouble: Maybe a mile ahead, emergency vehicles were parked along the shoulder, their lights flashing. Traffic on both sides was stopped as a tow truck backed up to an old Honda. Jay slowed to a stop, taking the opportunity to check things out without rubbernecking as a couple of guys in faded jeans attached chains to the Honda's front axle.

The ambulance had its lights off, and as he watched, the attendants lifted a gurney up onto the street behind the ambulance's open doors. A woman lay on it. He could tell by her ample figure, but her face was covered by the sheet. Jay shook his head sadly. Funny, though. The Honda looked shabby, but not battered.

A knock on his driver's side door interrupted his thoughts, and he opened it. "Hey, Dale," he greeted his friend. "Long time no see. What's going on here?"

Officer Dale Keun smiled slightly in greeting, but his eyes looked tired and the smile faded quickly. "Murder." He didn't seem to want to say any more, so Jay changed the subject.

"Wow. Uh, say, did you happen to catch that hunk of junk that flew by earlier?"

"What hunk of junk?"

"Oh, come on. He flew by me—must have been doing 90. It was…" He stopped as he realized that he couldn't even remember the color of the truck. "It was just a couple of miles back," he finished lamely.

"I must have missed him. I was, um." He grimaced and looked away, but Jay didn't need him to explain. Dale was still looking a little green.

Jay whistled. "That bad?"

"Worse. I won't be sleeping well for a while. Listen, there's a real sicko out there, and it's possible he's targeting people alone on the road. You pull in for the night, you find a nice crowded truck stop, or better yet, spring for a hotel, got it?"

Jay's thoughts flashed back to that creepy truck. "Hey, I'm always careful. I've got no illusions of being a tough guy."

"Good."

***

Seemed like a lot of people had crowded into the barbecue place—Long Pig or something like that. Jay hadn't looked too close at the sign. Long as it wasn't a chain, he didn't care. All he wanted was an excuse to sit down and maybe pretend he was hungry. And in a way he was—hungry for other people, that is. Food was another matter after what he had seen and heard that morning.

Dale hadn't given any details, but the radio was full of them: a vivid description of the murdered girl, how the person who'd found her had had to be sedated, guesses that the murderer was southbound... Jay kept waiting for his strange truck to be mentioned, although he couldn't figure out why.

Yep, it was company more than food he wanted. And if he was not mistaken, these other people felt the same way.

The girl who took his order looked like something from the menu herself. You could tell she'd been living on fried baloney and cornbread with plenty of butter. She waddled over to his table and gave him a big, gap-toothed smile. "What'll it be, hon?"

No beer, he decided regretfully. He ordered a coke and a barbecue sandwich. He could take the food along, he guessed. But he kept remembering his friend's face as Dale had told him about the murder.

"Sure 'nuff," the waitress said, giving him a porcine simper. Her short-skirted uniform strained over her mighty hams, and Jay looked away. Things were becoming surreal.

He thought he recognized a couple of people he had seen standing by the road—ambulance watchers. A lady in sunglasses kept telling her friend how awful it was as she ate French fries with plenty of ketchup. At the next table, a bearded black man looked back at Jay soberly. He was obviously listening to the conversation at his back.

It had taken an hour to get the traffic moving again, and a lot of vehicles had backed up on the road. The highway patrol had called in some special investigators, and they kept taking pictures and scraping blood off the highway until Jay was ready to tear out what hair he had left. After listening to the news with a horrified fascination, he'd managed to switch the station, which wasn't much better. Some oldie country station kept playing stuff like Ghost Riders. He wasn't ready to start driving again, though he'd be glad enough to get away from this place.

His order had come, and he was sipping the coke when a young guy came in. He looked like a refugee from a war or something. And when he ordered a beer, Jay knew right away he'd already had enough. He was, he told everyone at large, looking for the man who killed his wife. He had just been to identify the body. He drew an interested crowd right away.

Jay glanced at the black man who shook his head slightly. "They gonna run him in if he does any drivin' after this," the man said, and Jay nodded.

"They might run him in even if he doesn't do any driving," he said. Then, "Were you stuck in the traffic too?"

The other man shook his head. "I live up the road," he said. "Just came in to meet a guy about sellin' some steers."

"But you heard about the murder, I guess," Jay said. "They're saying her throat was all tore out—that she looked like a piece of meat."

"Yeah, I heard that. I heard that before."

Jay gave the man a sharp look. "What do you mean? Are you saying it's happened before?"

"I heard something before," the other man said. "Friend of mine—my cousin, in fact—told me about a murder down near El Paso. It was a few months back, and they didn't make so much fuss over it. I guess there was reasons."

Jay digested this. He didn't quite believe this guy, he decided.

At the other end of the room, things were getting lively. If that other fellow really was the victim's husband, he might have shown more decency. He was very drunk.

"I'm gonna park out there tonight," he vowed. "I got me a shotgun in the truck and the first bastard pulls up had better have a good reason for doin' it!"

"Uh oh," Jay said. "Sounds like someone's going to get his head blown off."

"If he don't shoot hisself by accident," the other man said. "But lead won't hurt that semi..."

For one vertiginous moment, Jay seemed to see again the truck that passed him on the road just before he came onto the accident scene. He shook his head.

"What semi?" he demanded.

Deep brown eyes met his own. "You know," the other man whispered. "I seen it on you that you knew."

Jay sat back, shaking. "I don't know what you mean," he said hoarsely. "What are you talking about?"

"You saw that truck. You just ask if anyone else saw it—you just ask!"

Jay gaped at him. "Black," he said. "Or maybe not. Maybe no color at all. It was speeding. I told the patrolman, but he hadn't seen it. It would have gone right by him! Right by where they had the road blocked off!"

The black man nodded. "I reckon she saw it too," he said.

For a long moment, Jay just sat there. "You're crazy," he said at last. "You're as drunk as that guy up front yelling."

The other man continued to watch him.

"LeRoy Bartlett," he said, extending one hand. "And I'm not drunk."

After a moment, Jay took the proffered hand. "Jay Carlson," he said. "And no, I guess you're not."

The drunk husband was finally convinced to sit quietly and drink his beer. Feeling the man's bleary and suspicious eyes on him, Jay got his sandwich to go and paid his tab quickly. He was afraid the guy might decide not to wait at the side of the road after all but pick out some poor sap to shoot right now.

But maybe things were okay—the huge waitress had leaned over the counter and was talking to the husband in sympathetic tones. Drunk and grieving as he was, he still managed to be downright focused on the opening of her shirt. Jay tried not to grimace as he passed by.

Once he was well away from the restaurant, Jay got on the CB and managed to get a hold of Dale, who was still on duty and kept a CB in his patrol car to keep track of Smokey reports that might give his position away. He told him about the guy in the restaurant. The drunk husband, that is; he didn't even want to think about the other guy. Gave him the creeps as bad as that weird truck.

"Great," Dale hissed in exasperation, static giving his voice a funny squelch. "That's the last thing we need. Thanks, Jay. I'll check up on him."

There wasn't much traffic on the CB, so he turned on the radio. Big mistake. The local station was fielding calls about the murder. Somebody—that LeRoy fellah, maybe—had called in to warn people about a mysterious old semi, which had stirred some ire among the legitimate truckers who lived in the area.

In an attempt to diffuse the time bomb he'd started, the DJ pulled out a song called "Truck Driving Vampire." It was a catchy tune and would have been funny, in other circumstances. As it was, Jay snapped off the radio, wishing he'd kept his XM radio subscription up to date.

Then there was nothing but the road and his thoughts. He reached for the sandwich, but the mangled beef in the rusty red sauce made his stomach lurch, and he tossed it out the window, littering laws be damned. In fact, he'd have welcomed a cop right then, even if it cost him a fine. He hadn't seen another car for over an hour.

Taking Interstate 10 into San Antonio, then I-35 to Laredo was beginning to sound like a good idea, even if it did add to his drive time. He'd lost a lot of time in New Mexico but nonetheless would welcome the noise and distraction of heavy traffic.

Once he'd put more distance between himself and the diner, however, things seemed better. He tried the radio and found a Classic Rock station with the funny commercials and no talk of mysterious killings. When he stopped at a gas station, he lingered a while talking with the pretty lady at the counter as she got him a couple of hot dogs and a Slushie. He tossed chips and a couple of candy bars on the counter next to a liter bottle of Coke, promising to eat better tomorrow.

Unlike a lot of attendants, she knew the area well and was full of light chatter about events. She was married with two kids, judging by the photo taped to the register, but she was friendly, and he found himself basking in her warm smile.

Her smile faded, however, when he asked her if she was driving home alone tonight. "Why do you ask?" she asked suspiciously.

"It's just that there was a murder last night, 'round Carlsbad. Woman alone on the road at night—"

"Oh!" She brightened. "Oh, you're so sweet. No, I'll be fine. My shift is off before sundown, and my husband comes to get me 'cause we've only got the one car. And Jerry has the place at night, and no one's gonna mess with him. Besides, that's in New Mexico. What are the chances he'll come around here?"

Her optimism was infectious, and when he got to the turnoff for 10, he blew right by it. She was right; what were the chances the murderer would stay on the same highway and go this far? Besides, he really couldn't afford the extra hours of driving through San Antonio. The station attendant had warned him that there was a big air show in Del Rio, and to be prepared for a lot of traffic.

True to her word, he hit Del Rio just at rush hour, with the highways full of tourists, military, and family in for the show. Even the drive-through at Arby's was backed up, but the crowds had succeeded in erasing the last of his earlier concerns. He even had a friendly argument with his swinging alien.

"Hey, it's a sandwich!" he told it indignantly. "Turkey, lettuce—it's healthy!"

He went on, stopping only for bathroom breaks and gas until the sun had set, and the world was lit only by a waning moon and the lights of his rig. Earlier that day, he would have been freaked at the thought of driving alone at this time of night. Now, he even had enough humor to chuckle as "Hotel California" came on the radio just as he was thinking about pulling in for the night. He'd only been on the road nine hours, but the events of the day had drained him.

He didn't have to turn in his load until late tomorrow morning, and besides, he was running low on fuel. He could turn in early, gas up, and get in as the warehouse opened. He rolled his eyes as the Eagles sang "Such a lovely place…" as he pulled into a truck stop just outside Eagle Pass.

Still, he was oddly relieved to find the place was called "Lazy T." He laughed at himself as he stuck his keys in his pocket and opened the cab door.

His laughter died in his throat.

It was the truck! It was parked just outside the glow of the parking lot lamppost, so that it was tantalizingly visible without having any clear features. But he knew it was the truck. He just knew. And all the horror of the morning came rushing back, leaving him frozen in his tracks.

Had it followed him? Ridiculous. It was already there when he pulled in. What reason did he have for thinking it was, well, after him?

Just call the cops, let them handle it, he thought. But what would he say? He had nothing to connect this truck with anything wrong, let alone a murder.

Screw it. Just put in an anonymous tip. Who knows? If that LeRoy character had heard something about it, maybe the authorities had, too.

Well, if he was going to call it in, he had better be able to describe it. The dim lighting made that harder than he'd expected, however. He couldn't tell the color, even if it was dark or light. He circled toward the back; the license plate was so dirty he couldn't even tell what state it was at this distance.

Oddly, he could see the mud flaps on the back wheels, which seemed to shine with an unearthly light. They had those silver silhouettes of a buxom woman reclining suggestively, but whether from shadows or road grime, their throats looked oddly incomplete.

That's sick, he thought, yet he found himself walking toward them, as if compelled to examine them more closely.

He suddenly realized he was angling toward the cab and not the back, remembered what Dale said about being alone after dark, and made a beeline for the truck stop. As he approached the doors, his eyes fell on the little Mexican guy who was sitting on the bench, holding some kind of beaded necklace and praying. For a minute, he had the urge to tell him to get inside where it was safe but brushed it off with a shake of his head. He was probably a beggar who was out there because the manager wouldn't let him in.

He never even looked up as Jay pulled the door open and stepped in.

The place had a dingy look that said it had seen better days, and it smelled like grilled food and overused bleach water. The sign said, "Please wait to be seated," but no one was at the counter. The pay phone was out of order, so he caught a busboy and asked him if they had a phone he could use.

"Sorry. Can't," he said dully. Either he didn't care why Jay needed the phone or he'd heard that request too many times to care.

"Listen," Jay spoke quietly, just in case the owner of the rig was in there eating. "I just want to call the police and report that old truck out there!"

"What? The red one? Hey, anyone own a big red semi?"

"That's mine," Jay hissed. Couldn't this kid keep his voice down? "The old one, over in the corner, just beyond the lights."

The boy made a big show of peering out the double glass doors. "I don't see no truck out there."

Jay looked. It was gone. "But... All right, who just left here?"

"Nobody."

"Don't give me that. Whoever was in that truck must have come in here—why else stop? Now I want to know who it was!"

The busboy just stared at him. So did some of the other customers. It was suddenly very quiet, the sizzle of the grill ominously loud. For a moment, he remembered the drunk husband back at the barbeque joint.

I probably sound as crazy as he did.

"Never mind," he mumbled and slunk out into the twilight before they called the cops on him.

Once he was out of the doors, he stopped dead, his jaw dropping. The damn truck was back! And it was turned around, so that the windshield now faced the restaurant. He caught a flicker of movement. Despite the distance, he thought he saw eyes...

Without realizing it, he was heading toward the truck, striding toward it, rolling up his sleeves as he went, his mind numb but for a sudden anger. *He's laughing at me! Who does this guy think he is, playing games with me? When I get over there, I'm gonna throw open the door, rip it off the hinges if I have to, then I'll—*

A hand caught him by the elbow. "Don' do it, mister."

Jay whirled, ready to take the head off whoever was coming between him and his target, and the moment he took his eyes off the windshield, his anger vanished, leaving a sudden panicked confusion.

What was he doing? He never started fights, and he'd actually thought of taking on a possible murderer? He'd been honest when he'd told Dale that morning that he wasn't a tough guy, and the thought of what he had been about to do left him weak-kneed.

He sank onto the bench beside the little Mexican who'd stopped him. Jay could feel his eyes on him as he tried to sort out what had just happened. Why had he thought there was someone in that truck laughing at him? Had he really thought he'd seen eyes? That'd be impossible—it was too far away, the light too dim. Yet...

He glanced up toward the truck.

"I would not look too closely," the man beside him warned. "That truck is old evil."

"You see it?"

"*Sí*. It has been here since you arrived."

"But when I asked in the restaurant, no one else could see it. Even I didn't for a minute."

The little man shrugged. Up close, he didn't look like the vagabond that Jay had assumed he was. He was clean and clean-shaven and looked well-enough fed. His face, illuminated by the lights outside the café, was gaunt, but from sadness rather than malnutrition, it seemed. Jay could see some kind of lace necklace with postage-stamp-sized pictures not quite tucked under his button-down shirt. His eyes regarded Jay steadily.

"Well, you're right, friend. That truck is old and evil."

"No. That is not what I mean. It's— *¿Como se dice?*—old... ancient. It is an ancient evil. You must stay away from it. Here." He kissed the beaded necklace and placed it in Jay's hands.

"Take it. Keep it close to you always. It will keep you safe."

"Uh, right." He glanced at it. The pretty jeweled beads were in groups, with a couple of links of chain and bead in between each group. Where they met was a medallion of a lady, then more beads, then a cross with a man stretched across it. A crucifix.

The word drudged up out of his memory. He'd been raised Southern Baptist, with a minister who had strong words about Catholics and their idols of the crucified Christ. Suddenly, things were getting surreal again.

He glanced back at the truck stop. He didn't think he could show his face in there again. Better to find something further down the road. He wasn't particularly sleepy anyway, especially not now.

He rose, again trying to look casual while feeling conspicuous. "Okay. Thanks. Listen, I need to be moving on. It was nice talking to you," he added, hoping he didn't sound like he thought the guy was crazy. Still—ancient evils and beads of protection?

He could tell by the man's look that he suspected what Jay was thinking. Nonetheless, he spoke seriously. "Keep those near you. And keep away from that truck. I will pray for you."

"Yeah, thanks."

He headed back to his rig without looking at the man or the battered old truck, though it continued to lurk on the edge of his vision. He reached into his pocket for his keys, unlocked the door, stepped inside, and immediately locked the door behind him. It wasn't until he moved to put the keys in the ignition that he noticed he still held the beads in that same hand.

He shook his head, now angry for how spooked he was allowing himself to get, and tossed them on the seat beside him. He pulled out of the parking lot resolving to find the next truck stop and get a good night's sleep.

In the meantime, put all this craziness out of your mind, Jay. This ain't some stupid horror movie where the monster is gonna jump out and eat you.

Still, it was several miles before he could steel himself enough to look in the rear-view mirror.

His one glance revealed an empty road, silvery in the moonlight, dark-edged with just that highway ribbon. It couldn't have been much past 10, but it felt later.

Jay looked down at the dash in front of him, lit palely, showing him all the dials, the radio, everything he might want to know about the safe little island that was his truck. He wondered what he would do if one of the warning lights came on. Check engine. Overheat. Gas...

Oh, shit! What in the name of God would he do? A cold sweat broke out on him and his hands trembled on the wheel. He felt the truck slowing down as he unconsciously eased up on the gas.

He glanced once more into the mirror and there, far back but coming up steadily were twin headlights. There was something ghastly about those lights, something cold and twisted—like phosphorescence on the waves of some dark ocean, where fishes nibbled at the flesh of the newly dead and lost sailors clung to spars, past praying, waiting for the dawn they would not see. He almost put on the brake.

This is crazy, he told himself. Get a grip! It's only a car. Or a truck? He decided to speed up a little. Time was money, he told himself crazily. Time—TIME!

And how old was that truck, anyway? And what was its story? How long since it had carried its last cargo—or did it carry something now?

Coffins, he thought and laughed a little at himself. What a load of manure he had been thinking!

He turned up the radio, and it was oldies. He didn't remember putting on that particular station, but then maybe he had outrun the station he had on earlier. Sixties stuff? Or older?

The lights were gaining.

He couldn't, he told himself, go any faster. You didn't speed a truck on a two-lane. Only a fool took those curves at seventy-five. A song ended, something about dead boyfriends, car wrecks, wailing laments from the dead. An announcer came on—or maybe it was just part of the song. He seemed to be reciting poetry.

Both hands on the wheel, Jay gave his attention to the road. Behind him, something big was gaining on him. Each time he rounded a curve, he lost sight of it and then as it came into view, it was closer. Closer—

"—and in the dark, moonlight is all, stars gleam above the clotted earth of opened graves, and we go down into the frigid dark, cold blood, cold kisses—"

With a squeal of brakes, he dragged the truck away from the verge. What a time to fall asleep! And how long had he been listening to that drivel on the radio? It was almost—he shuddered—hypnotic!

It's him talking! He's on the radio! Freeing one hand from the wheel, Jay reached over and switched off the radio, but the voice laughed. He turned off the CB. It had been nothing but static, anyway. The silence unnerved him, and he felt himself tense, waiting, anticipating the voice. He stared at the dial with something like horror. This could not be happening!

Behind him, the truck had matched speeds. It was playing with him, he thought. Waiting for him to stop of his own accord. Then it would pull up behind him, park quietly, waiting for him to open his door and—boots crunching on gravel—watching as the cab loomed up in front of him, beside him—his hand on the door handle—

"No!" He said it out loud. His knuckles were white on the steering wheel, clenched like the hands of a corpse gripped in rigor mortis. He felt the presence behind him, calling on him to pull over.

In one last effort, he switched on the CB and keyed the mike fast. "Mayday," he croaked. "Anyone there?"

"Ahead," a husky voice answered. "Keep comin', son. Don't let that thing make you stop. Just keep comin'." It was the voice of LeRoy Bartlett, the man he had met at the barbecue place.

He didn't even ask what he was doing, 400 or more miles south of Carlsbad, New Mexico, didn't ask what he thought he could do to help. He just set the mike down, put his hand back on the wheel, and prayed he could get to the friendly voice in time. Without thinking about it, his foot pressed a little harder on the accelerator. He took a turn a little too fast, felt the rig sway. The string of beads slid to rest against his thigh.

The engine sputtered.

"No!" He glanced at the gas gage. The red arrow hovered for a moment on the E, then sagged against the peg below it. "No!"

His truck slowed to a stop, and any hope of escape he may have had faltered with it.

He started to reach for his CB.

The lights in his rearview mirror flashed glaringly then faded as the truck pulled up beside him. Without meaning to, he glanced out his side window, at the darkness of the cab beside him. The driver, something, was there in the shadows. He could just sense it turn toward him—

And his mind went blank.

"Jay!" a voice squawked from his CB. "What's going on?"

A part of him wanted to answer, wanted to scream, but he couldn't make himself do either. Instead, his hands slowly fell from their death-grip on the steering wheel to his sides.

His fingers brushed against the chain of beads.

And his mind cleared. But just a bit, and he didn't know if it was his panic or his lack of faith that kept him rooted to his seat, as the truck pulled over ahead of him. Its door opened. He shut his eyes, not wanting to see what came out.

"Jay! Answer me! Where are you?" a voice called.

Using the hand that held the beads, he picked up the mike. "Help," he whispered.

He thought he heard boots crunching on gravel, but he couldn't tell over the pounding of his heart.

"Lock the doors, Jay. Don't let him in. He can't come in if you don't let him. I'm on my way."

What did he mean, he wouldn't come in? A strong swing with a crowbar and he could bust the window and force his way in. Jay could see it happening, heard the crashing glass. Of course, he could get in—

Of course, I can get in...

The crunching sounds had stopped. Did he hear another car, or was it the roar of blood in his ears? Why couldn't he move? The CB was silent now, just a steady sinister hiss. He was trembling so hard, he dropped the mike. The beads fell from his clutch but hung loosely from one finger. He couldn't take this.

You don't have to...

Any minute now, a crowbar—or maybe a shotgun. Our Father who art in heaven...

Of course, I can get in...

He was right by his door. Jay could feel it. What was he waiting for? Now I lay me down to sleep...

Why prolong this? Of course, I can get in...

I'll open the door, fast-like. Make a run for it. Jay felt his hand moving toward the door lock— the driver's side.

A part of him shouted, "No!"

Yes, unlock the door. Make a run for it. You can outrun me... Yes...

No! Clutching the beads again, he fought to stop his other hand. He was dimly aware of headlights reflected in the rear-view mirror lighting up his cab.

Better to run, a voice urged in his mind. Its voice. *Of course, I can get in. Better to open the door yourself and flee...*

His right hand pressed on the latch. His left hand punched it locked.

Open. The. Door! The voice commanded. His right hand obeyed.

A sudden dull thud, an inhuman screech of anger and pain, and the squeal of brakes.

Suddenly, whatever had a hold of Jay's will released him, and he sagged against the door, gasping. He screamed as the door was flung open and he fell into someone's arms. He struggled, pulled back a hand—the one with the beads—to punch.

"Wake up! It's me! I'm on your side!"

He stopped and blinked. The little Mexican from the truck stop was clutching his shoulders, shaking him. "What? How?"

"Get in! I explain later!" With a surprisingly powerful push, he shoved Jay into his car, slammed the door, then ran to the driver's side of the car and flung himself in. The engine was still running, and he threw it into drive and tore down the highway.

Jay risked a glance at the trucks stopped only halfway on the shoulder. Somehow it didn't seem so sinister anymore, just old and junky.

"Where's the guy? What happened to the guy?"

"Don't know," the man answered, "and I don' want to hang around to find out."

"But what if he comes after us?"

"He's not getting in this car. *Es consagrado*— you know, holy? He cannot come in, and as long as we stay in it, we're safe."

Nonetheless, his savior kept a close eye on the rear-view mirror.

Jay groaned and buried his head in his hands for a moment. Had he traded one lunacy for another? At least this one wasn't going to get him killed. Not yet.

He glanced up. "Look out!"

The little man turned his attention to the front just in time to swerve back into his own lane, narrowly avoiding the oncoming pickup. It made a sharp U-turn, flashed its lights, and laid on the horn.

"Don' look at it!" the little man warned, but Jay thought he'd recognized the driver.

"No, it's okay. It's LeRoy—he's, well, he was coming to help me! You got a CB?" Answering his own question with a glance, he turned the radio to the right channel and keyed the mike. "LeRoy!"

"Jay? Is that you in that El Camino? What the hell happened? Never mind. It can't be safe here. Follow me." And he pulled ahead. With a shrug, the little man complied.

They drove on in silence. After a few minutes, Jay was able to calm down enough to think about his rig. Should he call the state patrol and report it? On the one hand, he didn't want it tagged as abandoned and towed; on the other, he didn't want to do anything that might encourage someone to investigate it in the night.

In the end, he decided to wait. Maybe this LeRoy could shed some light on the situation, help him decide what to do.

One thing was for sure. He wasn't going anywhere near there until it was light. Daylight.

Mile markers flashed green in the glare of the headlights. Jay became aware that his right hand was sore. He held it up to realize he was still clutching the beads, the crucifix making a dull impression in his palm. The little man glanced his way. "El Rosario, it helped."

"I'm not sure. Maybe I didn't believe enough..."

"He believed. He was concentrating so hard on making you let him in, he never saw me." Jay saw him smile grimly in the light of the dashboard.

"I, uh, I don't even know your name."

"Miguel Felipe Eduardo Guiseppe de Aguilar."

"Miguel—thanks. You saved my life back there."

Miguel just nodded, but his smile softened.

They were silent again until LeRoy's voice came over the CB, instructing them to take a left. They pulled into a church parking lot. It was a small, adobe church, Catholic, Jay guessed, and he had only a moment to wonder why they hadn't gone to the police when LeRoy parked right up against the side of the building, dashed out, opened a door, and motioned them to follow him in.

Miguel had parked right behind him, inches off his bumper, so it was a short dash. Nonetheless, Jay's heart hammered in his chest, and judging from how the others were leaned against the wall catching their breath, he wasn't the only one.

LeRoy turned around and hit the light switch. The cheap bulbs filled the church with a low light. Behind the old worn pews were rows of plastic and metal chairs, and LeRoy turned one around and sat in it, motioning them to do the same.

"This is a mission church now, gets used once a month or so. Priest's a friend of mine," he said shortly. "Now what the hell happened?"

Jay didn't even know where to start. Fortunately, Miguel answered for them both, starting with how he'd followed the evil truck when it pulled out of the Lazy T and ending with ramming *el vampiro* with his car.

"I don't get it," LeRoy interrupted. "A car shouldn't have hurt it."

"Ah, but my car is special. *Es consagrado.* And I have a crucifix on the bumper."

LeRoy exploded into laughter. After a moment, Miguel joined him.

Jay looked at them with horror. Lunatics, he thought, I'm stuck in a church in the middle of nowhere with a murderer out there and lunatics in here.

"You are one crazy little Mexican!" LeRoy shook his head admiringly. "But that couldn't have stopped it permanently."

"*Sí*, but I had to do something..."

"Will someone tell me what's going on?" Jay finally exploded. "What are we doing here? Shouldn't we be going to the police?"

"The police can't help us," Miguel spoke reasonably, but Jay wasn't feeling reasonable. Nothing in this situation was reasonable—why should he be?

"What the hell's going on?" he screamed. It echoed in the empty church.

"Do you believe in the supernatural?" LeRoy asked grimly.

"No!"

"You do," Miguel said and for one crazy minute, Jay was remembering something he'd heard somewhere about how there were no atheists in fox holes.

How true, he told himself sententiously, and wondering how he'd fallen into this bizarre foxhole. He stifled a desire to laugh, knowing he wouldn't be able to stop if he did.

"Yes," LeRoy said softly. "You believe in evil, don't you, Jay? It's easier to believe sometimes than good. The evil that folks do when they's alive and the evil they leave after them—left over, you might say. Pure spite sometimes, like they can't just die and rest in peace." He shook his head. "That's it, I reckon. They don't always rest."

Jay shuddered. "You're spookin' me, man. I don't know what was out there, but you don't need to make it worse."

Miguel gave him a sympathetic nod. "He's no trying to scare you," he said. "He just starts where you are. You have seen what men should not have to see. It is real to you."

"Yeah," LeRoy took him up. "You believe in evil. But there's good out there too. Miguel here, I can see he's a Catholic. He believes in stuff like praying the Rosary and hidin' in a church. And I sure can't say he's not right."

"You brought us here," Miguel offered.

"Did, didn't I? I don't know...maybe you can throw a Baptist Bible at that guy out there. Been kind of scared to try—maybe he can't read, hey?"

Miguel smiled a little. "You have hunted too, I think," he said. "You have had dealing with this vampire before, no?"

LeRoy gave a grim nod.

"And maybe you learned that the old things, the old ways, they—they draw the lightning of God! True?"

For answer, LeRoy opened his shirtfront, revealing a crucifix and a medal both tied on the same string.

Jay turned his chair, looked up at the altar with its crucifix and statues and the large stained-glass portrait of Jesus. "That...guy... He's afraid of stuff like this?"

"He is," LeRoy said. "He's got the faith, that old boy."

Miguel chuckled. "And you," he said to LeRoy.

"Maybe," the other man said reluctantly. "Maybe. The jury's out on that one. My daddy would turn over in his grave if he ever thought his son would end up a Catholic."

"Mine too," Jay said, his eyes on the crucifix.

"It would be better," Miguel told him, "if this were a regular church. The Sacrament is not here."

"Priest bring it when he comes," LeRoy offered. "Gave me the key 'cause I clean up before monthly Mass. Doesn't know I use it for other reasons. Probably have me locked up if I told him about vampires."

"Too many do not believe," Miguel lamented. "Too many would make a new religion, they— *¿Como se dice?*—water down the old. At least we have the images of the saints. They will protect us."

"Okay," Jay interrupted, "so you're both vampire hunters. I'm in good company. But why me? Why's he after me?"

"We can't know that," LeRoy told him. "Why any of his victims? But you seen the truck."

"So did you—both of you!"

"And yet we live?" Miguel asked his unasked question. "God has permitted that we live to right this wrong."

"Reckon that's it," LeRoy agreed. "And now you too, Jay, whether you believe in Him or not."

Miguel was looking at the floor. "I hope I do His Will. I hope I hunt this creature because it is evil and not because I hate..."

Jay looked at Miguel questioningly.

"My sister," he answered, seeming smaller and older, though his eyes burned clearly in the dim light. "She married a gringo, moved to El

Paso. They divorced but she didn't feel she could come home. Stopped going to Church...

"She worked in a truck stop. She wrote me about a truck no one could see, how it frightened her. She called me one night, said she felt like it was waiting for her. Said she knew it was a *vampiro*, and that it knew she knew. She thought it was coming after her because she'd sinned...

"I thought she'd gone crazy. Loca. I told her come home." He let out a shaky sigh. "They found her body just across the border. They said it was a hate crime, but I knew. I've been looking for it ever since."

There was silence as Jay digested their words. He wanted to tell them they were crazy, wanted them to *be* crazy, but he couldn't. He'd seen too much, experienced too much that could not be explained. "So, what do we do?"

"He'll be coming for us," LeRoy said grimly. "Crucifix or no, hitting him with a car isn't going to stop him for long. And when he comes after us, he'll be pissed. Might affect his thinking. Three against one. I say we stop him here and now."

Three? Jay's inner voice squeaked, but he didn't say anything aloud. What was he going to do—take off on his own in the dark on foot?

"There is no Sacrament," Miguel lamented.

"But there's other stuff. Holy water. Icons. The Crucifix. Thank God the Bishop wouldn't let Fr. Tom replace it with some modern art rendition of the Holy Spirit."

"*Sí, gracias de Dios.*"

"What are you suggesting? A trap?" Suddenly Jay had a clear image of himself as the bait, like Shaggy in the old Scooby Doo cartoons. Only this time, he was sure there was no man in a creepy mask. *Zoinks.*

LeRoy slapped his hands against his thighs, the sharp crack of skin on denim echoing in the church. "Let's get moving. We got a couple of hours if we're lucky."

They set to work turning the neglected little church into a makeshift vampire trap. The legs of a couple of rickety tables in the vestibule were quickly and roughly carved into stakes. Each man stuffed one into his belt and the rest were set upon the altar. Pews were moved to barricade doors and create a path toward the altar.

There were no Missalettes—LeRoy said it was cheaper to just print the readings once a month—so they opened the music books to the Psalms and laid them face up on the seats.

LeRoy moved icons into protective positions while Miguel filled a chalice with holy water from the silver tank at the front of the church and poured it along the edges of their path. Jay was given the priest's holy water pot and sprinkler and told to sprinkle holy water everywhere outside the path.

"This really works?" he asked doubtfully as he worked his way along the right side of the church. He glanced fearfully at the stained-glass windows. The faces of the saints were still dark from the night.

Only behind the altar, at the low window bearing the image of Jesus who had rays coming from his heart like shafts of sunlight, was there any light, but Jay knew it was just the full moon setting. Would they survive until daylight?

"It'll burn him, even through his shoes. Won't stop him cold, but it'll discourage him."

Jay's hands trembled, nearly slopping the water. He tried to joke to cover his terror. "Maybe we should fill up some squirt guns."

Miguel gave him a dirty look, but LeRoy merely grunted. "There's an idea." He paused from where he had just dragged a chipped but very sturdy statue of St. Joseph into position on the left side of their trap. "Jay, help me with the Holy Family."

Jay set down the pot and stepped over the pews.

Suddenly, the window behind LeRoy shattered inward and a long piece of metal flew in. Its tip had been pulled and twisted like Jay's mother used to pull and twist yarn to thread a needle, and like that yarn through the needle, it went through LeRoy's shoulder. Its momentum pulled him to the floor and pinned him there.

"God!" he gasped and fell silent.

The improvised spear was followed by the vampire itself.

Jay shrieked and backpedaled, but Miguel ran between it and the unconscious LeRoy, shouting prayers in Spanish and flinging his chalice of holy water in the creature's face.

It gave a scream like a cross between a mountain lion and failing brakes and clawed at its face.

Miguel yanked the stake from his belt and stabbed hard, but the vampire twisted, and the sharpened wood scraped against ribs.

The vampire swung out with one arm and sent the little Mexican flying. He slammed against a pew, stunned, yet somehow still managing to murmur desperately under his breath, "*Ave Maria...*"

"Shut yer trap!" the vampire hissed with an incongruous Midwestern accent, but Miguel paused only long enough to say, "Jay! To the altar! *Corre!*" before turning his attention back to the advancing vampire.

Run. Great advice, yet somewhere between Jay's ears and his feet, something had short-circuited. He stood still, not even shaking, as his mind fought to resolve the conflicting images.

This could not be real! There was no such thing as vampires, and even if there were, this guy could not be it. He was balding, and, and he wore a stained white t-shirt and Levis that showed his plumber's crack not because it was trendy but because they didn't fit. His boots looked old and had a crack in the sole. He probably had on Wal-Mart tube socks for pity's sake! Who ever heard of a truck-driving vampire?

Yet he'd made a javelin out of a crowbar, jumped at least eight feet through broken glass. Miguel hit him with a car!

God, this can't be real. Wake up, Jay!

Again, an inhuman screech. Miguel must have stuck him with his rosary.

It wouldn't be enough.

Trembling again, Jay pulled out his stake and shoved it into the vampire's back.

The vampire spun, and Jay knew once and for all this was real, and if their attacker had ever been human, he was not so now. Its face had melted where the holy water had hit it, like a wax figure in the heat. Too much of the bloodshot eyes were exposed. The nostrils were elongated. The lips curved abnormally around vicious pointed canines. The chin was deformed, making his beard seem like a live thing scrambling for purchase. The front of his shirt was ripped as was the skin beneath it, but the blood was wrong—too pink and congealing.

Again, the command to run surged through his body, and again, Jay's feet seemed to miss the message. He could only manage a few stumbling steps back toward the altar.

He was going to die.

"Or not," the vampire answered his thoughts, its voice incongruously ordinary.

"What?"

"You, my friend, are a victim of unfortunate circumstances. I understand that. Been there myself. My argument ain't with you. So, I am willing to offer you a one-time deal."

The vampire advanced a step, but its manner was suddenly non-threatening. It even stuffed its hands into its pockets. Jay looked at its hands, then its chest wound, then its teeth. He stepped back some more, guided by the pew-lined path, determined to keep distance between the monster and himself.

"You are?"

The creature shrugged. "Sure. You leave. Right now. Go back to your truck. Finish your run. Then stay the hell off my highway. And I let you live."

It continued to advance, its movements casual, but clearly staying in the middle of the path. It stepped carefully over a hymnal that had fallen to the floor.

Jay's feet bumped against a step, then another.

"What about them?"

Jay backed into the altar, slid around it, terrified the entire time that the sideways motion would somehow break the spell and cause the vampire to lunge at his neck. He saw the stakes in front of him, but his hands were shaking so hard he knew he'd never be able to pick one up, much less shove it accurately. He thought of the others. He prayed the creature would say he'd let them go, too, and give him an easy out.

"You leave them to me."

"No." But he wasn't sure if he was turning down his offer or denying the reality of the situation.

The altar was bathed in colored light from the stained-glass window. He knew the light came from the moon, yet it was too bright; it was impossible. The whole situation was impossible.

"I don't believe this," he muttered, shaking his head.

The vampire's mouth twisted into a smile, though its eyes were cold and serious. "That's why you can't win. Those two—" He tossed his head contemptuously toward the wounded men behind him. "—they got faith. Truckloads of faith. That's why they've evaded me so long. And tonight's gonna take a while to get over."

He paused to push at the seeping flesh of his cheek, yet he was still smiling. "That LeRoy almost got me once or twice, too, don't mind telling ya. Gonna be a pleasure taking care of him."

"Why are you telling me this?"

"'Cause you ain't like them. You just don't have enough faith in God to go up against the likes of me."

Jay looked down at the altar, his eyes burning. His parents took him to Sunday services as a kid, but it never meant much, just what was expected. He never went now that he was an adult. Never even thought about it. The thing was right. He didn't have a lot of faith. Never did.

The vampire climbed the first step of the sacristy. "I'm giving ya one last chance. Go now."

He glanced at the thing's disfigured face. He might not believe much in God, but the thing obviously believed in His power. He grasped a stake in both hands. It was red and blue and gold in the light.

"No."

The vampire took the second step. "This is the last time I'm asking. Get out while the getting's good!"

And maybe even if he didn't have faith in God, God could have faith in him.

"No!" Jay shouted.

The vampire snarled like an animal and leapt.

Jay barely managed to lift the stake as it flew at him over the altar, hands outstretched, fingers curved like claws.

A shaft of light, suddenly bright and clear, shot from the heart of the stained-glass Jesus and illuminated the altar.

The vampire flew right into it.

There was sudden flare, like a nuclear blast, yet somehow as purifying as it was brilliant. The vampire's last screams reached a crescendo and disappeared with an anticlimactic pop. Then there was only the sound of human screaming.

After a moment, Jay realized it was him. Nonetheless, it took a moment longer before embarrassment overcame terror and he was able to close his mouth and look around.

He had flung himself backward into a wood wing-backed chair he guessed was for the priest and had curled himself tightly into it. Upon the altar and stretching out in front and behind it was a sickeningly human-shaped pile of ashes. One ash-covered stake was sticking straight up through what would have been the chest. The brilliant light was gone, replaced with the soft dimness of pre-dawn.

Jay uncurled himself and stumbled to the others. LeRoy was in bad shape, but the spear had missed the artery, and he was alive. Jay staggered to the holy water pot and sprinkler, grabbed it, and splashed some water on Miguel's face.

Miguel's eyes flickered open. He gasped in fear, saw it was Jay, and relaxed slightly. Then he looked at the altar, and his face broke into a small, weary smile. "It's over."

"You sure?" Jay was surprised how steady his voice was.

Miguel nodded. "We will dissolve as much of the ash as we can in holy water, scatter whatever we cannot. You, however, should go now."

Jay helped him stand and held onto him a moment until the dizziness passed and he assured him he was fine.

"LeRoy needs a doctor."

"*Sí*. There is a cell phone in the car. I will take care of that. You should go. You have done enough for us this night."

"I didn't do anything. It was all God."

Miguel smiled. "*Sí*. It always is. Now go. I have a can of gas in the trunk of my car. Your presence here will only complicate things."

"You sure?" Jay pulled the rosary off his neck. He held it out to Miguel. "Thanks, for, uh…"

Miguel closed Jay's hand over the beads and clasped his hand over it. "It is a gift. Take it and remember there are things which only God can do. *Dios te bendiga*."

***

An hour later, Jay was back in his rig, nursing it to the nearest gas station and doing his best to distract himself from dwelling over the night's events. As soon as he got his load dropped off, he was taking his earnings to the nearest bar and drinking himself silly, he decided.

Then an ambulance passed him in the opposite direction, its wail reminding him of the frailty and limitedness of humans. He glanced at the rosary which he'd curled around the base of his swinging alien.

Then again, maybe he'd just stop off at a church.

The Lobby

It was the later evening show, the later evening crowd—those who could not finish dinner and get ready in time and those who never worried about dinner and never knew whether they were ready or not. They came with their pimples and bubble gum, pierced lips and noses, long hair and shaven heads, girls in jeans and shorts and everything in between.

The gentleman observer was disgusted.

The gentleman had come to the theater with friends. His friends were people who planned things—usually with more care than they had planned this particular outing. The three—he and his companions—had been out to dinner and they had talked, and they had had dessert. And so they came to the late showing.

The gentleman seldom saw a new movie. He preferred to watch those he had collected over the years starring people he knew—Cary Grant, Joan Crawford, Jimmy Stewart—people who had been familiar to him for most of his life. They moved and spoke gracefully in black and white, and even in moments of high drama, they never forgot that essential decency legislated, it was true, but dependable, nevertheless.

But here the gentleman felt safe enough. Though he was a man of culture, he had been a lover of the fantastic for most of his life and—he smiled a little indulgently at himself as he admitted it—an avid reader of more than one author whose work his father would have consigned to the garbage can. To tell the truth, he had gone to see *The Mummy* and loved every minute of it. There was no reason he should not risk seeing the sequel.

The tickets were bought, candy and popcorn as well, and all three found seats. He must brace himself for the previews—times had changed, after all. But the volume of sound took his breath away. It had done so before. This was a far cry from the cartoon and newsreel of his youth.

Alas, the end of these advertisements—for remarkably worthless movies—brought no relief. The main attraction did not please him. One knew, one had been told from time to time, that a "return of" movie was often inferior to its progenitor. But this specimen seemed to him so very disappointing that the gentleman could not keep his seat. Excusing himself, he left his companions to enjoy themselves, if they could, while he betook himself to the lobby.

The lobby was a show in itself as the latecomers drifted in. These modern people seemed as bizarre to him as the characters on the screen. He seldom came out in public at this hour, and he wondered mightily whether that much-tattooed young man worked in a factory by day, or whether the damsel in black—even to her lipstick and fingernail polish—might be the same lady who cashed his checks at the bank. Perhaps she took the ring from her lip during working hours?

And so he sat, glancing at his watch from time to time, watching this other show. Once in a while, he looked over at the candy counter, where a young man with a ponytail dispensed his overpriced wares. In a booth the ticket seller sat, small and gnarled, his face reflecting some twisting that might also show in his body if he rose from his chair. He turned a bright-eyed gaze on the gentleman and smiled. It was not a reassuring smile.

The gentleman glanced at his watch. Barely ten o'clock. He drummed his fingers on one knee. He did not smoke—and very likely in this new and vulgar world, smoking would be the one thing prohibited. Probably the only thing— unless you counted prayer.

The people who came in were more and more strange. A couple in evening clothes—but where had he seen such clothes save in an old illustration?—approached the ticket seller. The gentleman could not hear all that was said, but he could have sworn the man was talking

French. Arm in arm, the pair moved off into the arch and disappeared. He wondered which of the mediocre offerings they had chosen to view.

A crowd of college boys came in. At least he thought they were from the college. All wore long hair, unwashed, and in one case, braided. There were beards, coarse and dirty clothing, and footgear of a sort he had not seen before. No one wore jeans, and though there were wristbands and neckbands in plenty—gold, by the look of it—he saw none of the bizarre face piercings he had observed in the earlier crowd.

These, too, after a whispered parley with the ticket seller, disappeared. They, he concluded, would probably enjoy the mummy's return. A few more people came late—to his annoyance, his watch seemed to have stopped—a down and outer in a very out-of-date suit, two youngsters in costume with pantaloons and swords, a veiled lady who glanced behind her furtively as she spoke rapidly in a foreign language to the ticket taker. It was a parade, the like of which, he had never imagined could occur in his city—or anywhere else except New York, perhaps, or LA.

During a lull in business, the ticket seller glanced over at him again, his smile more inviting, one crooked hand beckoning slightly. Reluctantly and rather stiffly, the gentleman rose.

"Good evening," the gentleman said. "I am afraid I did not enjoy the movie. I am waiting for my friends."

He wondered why it was he felt he must explain himself. But the ticket seller seemed sympathetic. "I can understand that," he said, and his voice was smooth and husky at the same time. "Perhaps you would like a refund?"

The gentleman was startled, but he did not show it. "As a matter of fact, I would," he admitted. "*The Mummy* was pretty good, but this…"

"Ah yes." The ticket seller chuckled. "The first movie reminded you of your youth."

The gentleman did not quite answer this. "It was good, clean fun," he said.

"I'd imagine," the ticket seller said, as he handed over the refund, "you'd like to go back to the days of double features. Boris Karloff in his prime. Bela Lugosi."

The gentleman took out his wallet, accepted the bills. "One realizes that time and society change," he said hesitantly. "But it seems to me we have lost more than we have gained."

"People are more shallow?" the ticket seller suggested. "More coarse?"

"That, certainly."

"This world," the other man said dreamily, his eyes focused somewhere above an unspeakably garish poster, "is a very interesting place. There is more than meets the eye—more than men know."

"One hopes so."

Again, that chuckle. "I wasn't speaking metaphysically," the ticket seller said. "I was speaking quite prosaically. Your friends came to be entertained—and we do not let them down. But there is more to life than entertainment."

"You could hardly offer a philosophical lecture at a movie theater."

The ticket seller leaned back, showing that there was indeed a cruel twist to his spine. "No, that would be expecting too much. But there are dreams and there are dreams. Tawdry ones, serious ones—and there are different levels of satisfaction."

The gentleman nodded. "That couple—the ones in evening clothes," he said. "What movie were they going to see?"

"Oh, I am afraid their dreams were of the tawdry sort." The old man shifted in his seat, a moment's physical pain drawing up the corners of his mouth in a brief, sardonic grin. "She, you know, is married to someone else. Someone who would have a great deal to say about this night's work—if he knew."

"They spoke French."

The ticket seller nodded.

"Those college boys?"

"They were not college boys. They were not boys at all. They were...explorers, you might say."

At this, the gentleman raised his eyes—for he was a highly intelligent man—and looked square into those of the ticket seller. "I see," he said.

"And the others—all have needs. Needs that go beyond what a theater can ordinarily offer. Low desires, higher ones... What you might call aspirations, though true aspirations are satisfied elsewhere. Even plain curiosity. It is the hour," the other man added, smiling his unsettling smile, "when dreams come true."

The gentleman looked at his watch. "I see," he said again. The hands had not moved. It was still ten o'clock.

The ticket seller waited. There was no hurry.

"And what," the gentleman asked, "is the cost of a ticket?"

"Not so very much. Something you will not miss. Something you never asked to have and will soon forget."

The gentleman gazed at the counter, thinking of his father and his mother. Of Saturday matinees, of well-known streets and shops and friends. Of a world, frightening enough, he supposed, but familiar and safe for all that. Of landmarks of the soul...

Of choices that might have been.

The ticket seller moved slightly, making a small noise as he eased himself in the chair.

"They all paid?" the gentleman asked. But he was thinking of the world he had known and the world that was now. What had gone wrong?

Was it merely that he had grown older? Had he failed somehow to adjust, to fit in?

Or, and this was more disturbing still, had he by his very careless happiness in the past failed those who were born after him? He had never married. He had no children of his own. But were not these youngsters, these wasters of time and mind and—and of heart and soul— were these not his children by the very fact that they inhabited his world and had come after him?

"Yes," the ticket seller said, and he was no longer smiling, "they all paid. It isn't much."

"And when I went into the movie," the gentleman asked, "it wouldn't be the same movie? It wouldn't be a movie at all?"

The ticket seller nodded. "It would be as it should have been. As you remember and desire."

"As I desire?"

"Precisely. You might have a very happy life."

"I might use my youth with an eye to the future. Might prepare myself better to serve these who suffer the results of my generation's negligence and folly?"

The ticket seller frowned. "You needn't think of the future at all," he said. "You could be happy."

The gentleman straightened himself, put away his wallet. "Thank you for the refund," he said. He glanced at his watch. It was ten o'clock and the ticket seller was closing his booth.

The gentleman walked over to a bench and sat down. Around him, the present glared and flashed in all its pathos. In a while, his friends would emerge, dazzled a bit, probably criticizing the movie, but not sorry to have spent their evening here. Something in them would have been refreshed even by this poor effort at childish fun.

He, too, was refreshed. Life was, as the ticket seller had said, far greater than men knew. Yet just as certainly there was more to life than that poor, crippled creature could comprehend.

But here, the gentleman considered, he misjudged. He looked somberly at the empty booth. Would not an angel, even fallen, know about eternity?

Accidental
Undeath

"Oh, God, please, please don't die!"

I held her broken body in my arms and tried desperately to remember first aid, but I couldn't seem to get past "check for breathing." She was breathing, sort of ragged breaths interrupted with a bloody cough. The middle of the night, on this damn dark highway, there was no help for miles around.

A part of my mind kept saying I should go back to my rig, grab my phone, call for help, but the rest of me was frozen, caught up in a myriad of emotions: panic, guilt, fear...

...hunger-lust as I smelled her blood.

Even as I cried and begged her to live, I could feel my canines growing. I hated being a vampire!

It was a moonless summer night like this one, almost five years ago. A vampire with a sick sense of humor heard a Michael Longcor song about a "Truck Driving Vampire" and thought it'd be cute to fly into my cab and latch onto my jugular. I keep a stake under the seat in case I run into her again.

Still, after five years, you start to adjust, you know? Even try to find some fun in your nosferatu abilities. That's what I'd been doing, drivin' my overnight run on a lampless highway, headlights off, trusting to my heightened night vision and singing "Midnight Cowboy."

The song had ended, I'd looked down to pick a new song, when all-of-a-sudden I heard a scream and squeal of brakes, and my rig did a horrible sideways lurch. I hit the brakes—too late. I heard glass breaking and metal screaming. Metal, but not human anymore.

I shoved open my door—I was fine, thanks to my vampire state—and ran around to the other side. I saw a Mustang Convertible half-shoved under my rig. I'd already drug it half a block before my truck skid to a halt. I found the driver, a pretty little thing, draped over her dashboard, no seatbelt. God only knows why she hadn't flown through the windshield and smashed into the trailer.

Had she even seen me? I looked at my black cab and trailer. She hadn't seen me. I cursed the darkness, my own stupidity.

Like some kind of idiot, I brushed back her blond hair, dabbed at the bleeding cuts on her face.

I had cleared away the glass—my cuts were already healing—and had pulled her out, only remembering afterwards that you're not supposed to do that. Now she lay, rag-doll limp, in my arms, blood dribbling from her lips.

That happened on those late-night war movies when someone punctured a lung. Did she puncture a lung? Did I do that pulling her out? Or did it happen when she smashed into me?

Why did it have to smell so good?

She looked so young, maybe 17. What was she doing out here at this time of night?

All alone, so young, her blood so fresh...

I was getting dizzy, kind of drunk with shock and desire. It wasn't like the kind of desire you surmise from those Dracula movies. It was more like waving a steak at a wild animal. You know, more feral.

Feral. That was the word she used when she'd tried to explain turning to me.

"Don't believe all the folklore about us vampires," she'd said as we sat drinking in some sleazy bar on the bad side of New Orleans. It was an hour or so after she'd bitten me, in bat form, for the first time. I'd come to with my head on the steering wheel, and my cab wrapped around some huge old tree. Naturally, the trooper didn't believe my story, thought I was DUI.

As I pulled out my wallet to give him my license, a note dropped out, just a picture of a bat, the words "Questions? Meet me at," and an address. So, there I was drinking white wine—

she refused to let me have a beer—with this striking lady dressed in black, with white lace, and wearing heavy dark make-up.

Yeah, it's a cliché, but she seemed to go for that stuff.

"Some of it is true," she'd remarked as she took a sip of wine. She was being all conversational. Me, I was humoring her, hoping she'd let something slip that I could use to sue her for repairs to my rig. I thought she was a crazy Goth. I had no idea what I was up against.

She continued, "The aversion to sunlight, the budding canines… You'll find out as time goes on. The blood, well, it's like alcohol. There is fine champagne, and there is"—she curled her lip— "beer. You would probably be satisfied with eating your hamburgers blood rare."

She'd been right, too. Until now. Hunger was starting to win over panic as I fought to remember what my too-long-ago Red Cross class had said about internal bleeding. Get help. I had to get help. But who?

I couldn't call the state troopers; ol' Smokey would want to hold me for questioning, probably in the morning. I still have a scar on my hand from when a beam of sunlight came through a crack in the curtain in that hotel where she'd turned me. I would not survive a sunrise in a jail cell. No, local authorities were out.

Unless... Were there any hereabouts who were turned, too? I'd met one or two troopers who'd been bit. It wasn't easy for them, keeping a job like that, but a few managed. I'd always just bump into them by accident, usually on the wrong side of a speeding ticket, and they'd laugh in my face when I'd try a little nosferatu mind-control. How would I find one now?

Damn, if I only had access to the Internet. The only thing she'd left me after turning me was a message scrawled on the mirror in lipstick: a web site and a password. There's just about everything a vampire could need on that site, from survival tips to chat rooms to e-mail addresses of doctors searching for a cure and who'll give you doctor's orders to get out of daytime activities—something that's come in handy when I've had to go to court over alimony and such.

Anybody can add information; I've got a blog on the best all-night diners and gotten a few folks connected with trucking firms that hire for nightshifts only, no questions asked. Maybe someone there would know a local who would help. But I didn't have a connection. I—we—were alone.

I could go for help. I couldn't transform like others could—never tried, it just weirds me out too much—but with my vampire strength, I could pull her car out, drive to the nearest town—it's what? 20 miles or so away? I could dump her at a hospital. I could—

I couldn't. She'd die before then if I moved her more, and I couldn't leave her alone.

I'd been alone so often. It stinks, even when you're alive. I hadn't noticed it as much when I was young and first starting out. I'd loved the long hauls, just me and the road. Then the nights in hotels or in the sleeper of my cab started getting old.

Then came the day I saw JoAnn, leanin' against a hot red car. Hot was the word. Hot engine spewing steam; hot pants making me steam. I couldn't stop fast enough. I took her the 200 miles to her new job, wasn't even on my route. Started finding routes to take me near her, then found a job hauling gas around to local stations.

Bought her a ring, said "I do." Little house—even the stupid white picket fence, felt like I was livin' some romantic country song. Then, just like a song, job goes bad, things get sour, she changes the locks, and I'm doing scab jobs for UPS to pay alimony. Then, if that wasn't enough, some damn vamp decides it's funny to make a truck-driving vampire.

Now, I'm kneeling on the highway, praying over some strange girl who's going to be dead thanks to this truck-driving vampire, and I don't even know if God'll listen to me anymore.

"You can't die. Just hold on, honey. I'll think of something!"

I have to chance putting her in my cab, drive her to the hospital or a hotel or somewhere they can get her help. It can't be any worse than leaving her, right? Then I'll just use a little mind-control, so they forget me.

Who was I kidding? I never was very good at that, as my driving record will show, and what if there was more than one person around? Even if I could make them all forget me, it'd take too long. Besides, it's one thing to forget a common garden-variety speeder; it's another to forget a guy carrying in a girl who's all hurt and bleeding. All that blood.

All that blood...

Oh, my teeth hurt. I was salivatin', getting really heady. All that blood... I'd never bitten a human, but now, oh...

I could turn her.

I could bite her, three times—that myth was true—and save her.

How long did I have? I remember she had said you had to take your time with turning. "It's not like Thanksgiving, where you glut yourself then sit like a bloated whale in front of the TV," she'd said. "It's a feast of the senses, all of them. You need to feel your victim, smell him, savor his taste, open yourself to him as you take him within you. After each experience, there must be time for the hunger, the need to build again. This isn't a matter of feeding; there's a synergy, an intertwining of essence. A turning cannot be rushed."

I didn't know if she'd said all that because it was true or to get me hot, to lure me to her hotel room. How much mind control had she done on me? It probably wouldn't have taken much. She was pretty, in a Gothic sort of way, and I'd been so lonely—

I don't have time to think about that! Think back to the turning. How long had it been between the second and third bites?

The young girl stirred slightly in my arms. Was it shock? Fear? She'd never opened her eyes. Did she somehow know what I was, anyway?

"It's okay, honey. I'll take care of you. I promise."

I would, too. No way I'd screw her like Vampira screwed me, leaving me with the curtains drawn and that cryptic note on the mirror. God, what a shock those first weeks had been, until I'd found others like me. No, I'd take care of this little lady from the start, teach her about her new life, take her with me on hauls until she'd learned enough and was ready to go on her own. Who knows? I'm an okay-lookin' guy and I won't get any older. Maybe she'd stick around awhile. Maybe....

I'd have to get some dirt from here, put it in the cab for her. Then I'd take her somewhere, probably someplace isolated. She'd panic at first. I did. I'd make her understand, sure I could.

Then we'd figure out what we'd tell her parents. If we told her parents. I haven't told nobody, just keep makin' excuses, moving on when someone got too nosy. Haven't been home in five years, even missed grandma's funeral. Went to the gravesite by night, but no one knew. Mom's still angry. And JoAnn—she thinks I hate her, the way I keep doin' stuff through a lawyer, never wantin' to see her face-to-face.

"Have you got family? A boyfriend? Honey, what do you want me to do?"

Her shuddering stopped. She ain't going to make it. God, she ain't going to make it.

I licked my lips, cut my tongue on my teeth. She wouldn't be the same, but she'd be alive, in a way. That was better than dying, wasn't it?

Wasn't it?

The Women of Rattlesnake Hill

They began calling one another early in the morning, the women of Rattlesnake Hill, soon after the menfolk had eaten their eggs and grits and biscuits with homemade sausage and gone to the fields.

It began at the Tuckers' house when Brandi Sue woke up tired and sick and dream-dazed. Her mother took one look at her face, the color of unwashed bedsheets, her eyes wild with memory and longing, and knew she'd better call Aunt Opal right away.

And so, while the men were spitting tobacco with the taste of breakfast still in their cussing mouths, and their tractors hummed or roared or sputtered and stopped—all but Buster Herndon who still plowed with a mule—the women gathered at the Tuckers' house.

The girl had nothing to say as she lay half-scared but smiling—and oh, the horror of that smile!—with her eyelids drooping as though she would return gladly to her dreams and surface no more.

Aunt Opal sat herself in the living room rocking chair. Plump and cowlike Aunt Ruthie sat on a kitchen chair beside her.

Aunt Opal stared grimly out the window while she rocked, squeak-thump, squeak-thump, her big-knuckled hands on the arms of the chair. Mrs. Tucker—Mary Jo, that was—watched her anxiously from the kitchen doorway, a tentative cup of coffee in one hand. The other women, about a dozen of them, were scattered between the two rooms.

"Reckon we got trouble again," Willa Mae Quarles whispered to Grandma Tucker who sat beside her on the couch. "Reckon it's like before."

The old lady nodded, tears of helplessness gathered in her eyes, steaming up her glasses. "That pore child."

"She won't know," Willa Mae said. "We can make it right."

"Until she dies," Grandma Tucker reminded her. "But what if we're all gone to glory ourselves by then? What if there's no one that knows to do for her? What if she lives to be a real old lady, maybe, and then turns into—"

"There'll be someone," Willa Mae said stoutly. "We'll see to that."

"And who do you reckon done it?"

Willa Mae was silent.

"Talmadge done it," another voice cut in. "You seen him—his cheeks pink and his lips red. They don't fix them up that good at the funeral parlor."

"Reckon it was!" Cora Bea Waters said excitedly. "He didn't look like no heart patient. And all them years, none of us knowin'—"

"Hush up!" Aunt Opal said suddenly, glaring at the group of ladies. "He's your own uncle, Cora Bea, whatever he's become. It ain't his fault."

"Sure ain't," agreed pillowy Aunt Ruthie, echoing her more forthright sister.

"But what are you saying?" Mrs. Tucker wailed. "Aunt Opal, what are y'all saying about my pore little girl and—and—" She broke down sobbing while the coffee splashed a tan stream on her white flowered apron.

"Reckon you know, Mary Jo," Aunt Opal said flatly, and Mary Jo Tucker's narrow, worn face went white. "Reckon you heard about the last time we had trouble like this."

"Twenty years back," Grandma Tucker said faintly. "It were Mary Harper, your husband's cousin."

"She was young, wasn't she?" Cora Bea said in her nerve-skittering voice. "Got kilt in a car wreck with my Uncle Lonnie—"

Aunt Opal glared at the younger woman and Cora Bea subsided.

"I—I wasn't listening too good," Mary Jo said faintly. "What do we do?"

"We do like we've always done," Aunt Opal said. "We get us an ashwood stake about a foot and a half long, and some garlic—which I've already brought—and we put him to rest."

"You mean dig him up?" Mary Jo gasped. "But he was buried way last Monday week. He'll be all stinky."

"No, he won't. Not if he's the one."

"And that's really what you done with Mary Harper? Put a stake through her heart?" Cora Bea shrilled. "Just like in the movies?"

"Cora Bea," Aunt Opal said with measured emphasis, "reckon you could help out some? Do Mary Jo's breakfast dishes, maybe?"

Unabashed, the younger woman flounced into the kitchen. She wore makeup, and her rose colored stretched pants were too tight for her generous bottom.

"Now then," Aunt Opal went on in a lower voice, "it was me and Ruthie here and Deannie Perkins who's dead now, done the job last time. But I reckon some of y'all might have been there." She peered around the room. "You, Esther, and you, Ruby. And Grandma Tucker, of course."

The last-named lady made a small whimpering sound, quickly suppressed. Aunt Opal ignored her.

"The way we done it—the way it's always been done, I reckon—is the one whose closest kin are in danger, that one has to drive the stake." She trailed off, musing. "And some of the younger ones better come along to dig."

Mary Jo Tucker gave up all pretense of serving coffee and stood clutching the pot with both hands, her mouth working as though she might throw up.

"Mary Jo," Aunt Opal said sharply, "if this ain't done, your daughter might well die. Next time he gets to her maybe. And then she'll come back. She'll wake up just like Talmadge done."

Mary Jo nodded weakly. "And if we—if Talmadge—"

"If we send Talmadge to his eternal rest," Aunt Opal said, "your girl will be just fine. She'll live out her life and never remember any of this."

"And when she finally does die—of natural causes, I mean—what then?"

"When she does, someone will fix her up, so she doesn't come back. Like we done the others that's been touched by this plague. We just missed Talmadge somehow."

"You cut off their heads, don't you?" Cora Bea called over the clink of dishes. "And stuff their mouth with garlic. It was on the late show."

Mary Jo Tucker groaned and slid partway down the wall. She looked like she was going to faint.

But Aunt Opal wasn't going to cut her any slack. "You go out and check up on all the kids, Cora Bea," she said. "When you get done with those dishes, I mean. And see if Mary Jo's garden needs weeding."

She turned to the others. "Who'll come?" she asked.

Tammy Quarles would come. She was young and strong and not pregnant yet. Linda Tucker and Jeannie Waters—she was Cora Bea's sister-in-law—and Aunt Opal and Aunt Ruthie, and of course, Mary Jo Tucker.

"But I won't dig up no body," Mary Jo moaned when she could speak. "Why can't the menfolk take care of it? Send for the preacher maybe."

"Mary Jo," Aunt Opal said sharply, "you wasn't raised here on Rattlesnake Hill, so we'll let that go for this once. But I'm telling you now that this here's women's business. We don't tell the preacher neither. He might say it's heathen stuff—Catholic even. But we know better."

"Maybe it is heathen stuff," Mary Jo said sullenly. "I never heard of such nonsense."

"It ain't nonsense and you know it. It's been goin' on here since the hill was first settled, way back in 1810. Just one more curse brought over from the old country, I reckon. Like so many of our children bein' born cross-eyed or prone to nosebleed."

Grandma Tucker pressed her dried-up old lady lips together. "Ain't nobody but got some kind of troubles to bear," she said.

"Shall we go now?" Aunt Ruthie ventured. "We want to be back before dinnertime."

Aunt Opal rose decisively. "Fetch some shovels and a crowbar, Mary Jo," she said. "And stop that sniveling." She reached down for the sack of fresh pulled garlic she had brought and, beside it, the stake.

"You other women work out who's to cook extra for dinner," she ordered. "Don't want the menfolk gettin' curious."

She marched out the door and her chosen band followed. They met Mary Jo near the barn and threaded their way carefully among the corn, cutting across to the Rattlesnake Hill Church of Christ.

"It's a good thing there's honeysuckle all over the fence. No one can see us from the road," one of the young ones said.

"Ain't hardly any traffic out here anyway," Aunt Opal replied, stumping doggedly between the rows. She would need her liniment tonight, she thought grimly, wincing at the pain in her hip.

They came up beside the small, clapboard structure and filed silently into the graveyard. There was only one grave not grassed over.

"We can wet it down when we're done," Aunt Opal said with satisfaction, "and none the wiser. Brother Lynch has done left the sprinkler hooked up."

They began to dig, moving the dirt aside into a neat pile. "I forgot," Aunt Ruthie said, "how much dirt it takes to fill up a grave."

"Reckon they don't need to plant folks so deep," Aunt Opal grumbled. "It ain't as if we got wolves no more."

"Not since Cousin Andrew," Aunt Ruthie said. "And we had to melt down our grandmother's best salt and pepper shakers to make silver bullets."

Aunt Opal frowned. "We done had our share of afflictions, now you mention it."

"I hit something," Tammy said, interrupting the aunts' reminiscences. "Reckon it's the coffin?"

"Don't say that word!" Mary Jo gasped, dropping a bucket full of dirt. "Oh God," she moaned. "What am I doing here?"

"Reckon that's it," young Linda Tucker said. She began to clear the lid. "Shall I break this here lock thing?" she asked Aunt Opal.

"Go ahead," Aunt Opal said. "If you're strong enough."

"I'll help her," Tammy volunteered and applied her own brawny strength. Something gave with a dull, splintering rip. "Damn! Broke a fingernail."

"Tammy! For shame. Swearing—and in the churchyard too!"

"Sorry, Aunt Opal," the girl said, blushing a little. "Reckon we can get the lid up now."

There were more wrenching sounds from below. Presently, the others peered down at the ruddy-cheeked figure in the coffin. Tammy balanced precariously on the top edge of the wood, and Linda actually stood on the corpse's legs. "He don't look very dead, do he?" she said.

"There's blood on his mouth," Tammy murmured in disgust.

"It ain't his fault," Aunt Opal told her severely. "We come here in kindness, not hatred."

"How's Mary Jo goin' to get to him?"

"She'll have to sit on his, er, lower parts," Aunt Opal said. "Help her down."

Mary Jo, unable to take her eyes off those red-stained lips, allowed herself to be handed down by her more hardy neighbors. Aunt Opal gave her the stake and hammer, and Tammy helped her to center it over the heart.

She struck a feeble blow and felt the corpse quiver beneath her resting knees.

"Hit it harder," Aunt Opal said. "Don't be a-scairt."

Mary Jo struck again with no more result than before. And then suddenly, he smiled up at her, this Talmadge who had sung off-key in church, who always had tobacco juice dripped on his collar, who had once driven an old black pickup on the Rattlesnake Hill Road.

He opened his eyes and smiled a ghastly, seductive smile, and she smelled the smell of his mouth like blood and something rotten. Like cleaning a chicken on a summer's day.

She clenched her jaw and struck with all her strength. This time, the blood welled up, staining his white shirt, smearing her hand where she held the stake.

"I'm killin' somebody," she whispered. "I'm flat out killin' a man."

His smile grew brighter, red lips lifted to show delicate, gleaming fangs. "He didn't have no teeth before," she told herself firmly. "Not but a few stumps."

Again, she struck.

The body jerked obscenely under her and one of her legs slipped sideways so that she straddled his hips, her blue jeans stretching as she felt the corpse move horribly beneath her— heavy, leather belt, scratchy old man's Sunday suit—and in the midst of her revulsion, she was filled with sudden pity. It was not Talmadge she struck—it was the devil! It was the devil who roused those who should have slept and made them do things they never would have done otherwise.

And this time, when she hit the stake, something gave mushily beneath, and blood gouted from the still smiling mouth. The body quivered in one last rictus and was still.

Mary Jo climbed heavily to her feet, tired and exalted at once. She let Jeannie and Aunt Opal pull her from the hole. When she reached the clean grass, she sat down and sobbed with relief. Aunt Ruthie would have come to her, but she shook her head. "I'm alright," she got out. "Alright—"

Silently they filled in the grave, after Aunt Opal's garlic had been put in place around the now rapidly deteriorating corpse and stamped down the dirt. Then they turned on the sprinkler for a few minutes to smooth it out.

"Looks about like it did," Aunt Opal decided at last. She pulled an old watch from the pocket of her lavender-flowered dress. "Almost dinnertime," she said. "Let's get back and wash up."

"What about my girl?" Mary Jo said now. "Will Brani Sue be alright now?"

"She'll be fine," Aunt Opal told her. "After what you done—"

Slowly Mary Jo managed a smile. Yes, her daughter would be fine. And one day, they or their descendants would take care of her when she died for real and make sure she never ended up like poor Talmadge.

That's how it was with the women of Rattlesnake Hill. They took care of things. That's how it had always been.

My Big, Fat Zombie Wedding

The bright Louisiana sunlight shone through the diner windows, making Vida long to head home and go to bed. Night shift at the museum could be brutal. However, Stella had called her just before she'd gotten off work and told her she had big news—news that would change Vida's life.

"I have found him!" she'd declared.

Now, Vida sighed and studied the coffee in her cup before addressing her friend. *I should have ordered a double espresso instead of decaf. Fatigue. That's the only reason I'd consider going on a blind date.*

"Come on, Stella: 'Great personality'? You know that's the kiss of death, right?"

Stella arranged her many silk scarves and wagged a jeweled hand at her.

"Darling," she said in her mystical French Quarter accent, "you told me yourself you wanted a quiet man, good listener, great personality, and looks were not important."

Vida frowned. At forty-two and forty pounds overweight, a small-town girl new to the big city, she was finding her choices limited. Still...

"Lay it on me. How bad is he?"

Stella laughed. "Oh, but you underestimate me! He is an older man, but very well preserved. Easy on the eyes, I promise you.

"Okay. Then what's wrong with him?"

Her friend gave an airy shrug. "He...has an odor; it's inherent to his condition."

Vida bit her lip. "Condition" was the polite way of saying "paranormal." She'd met a lot of paranormals, and they all seemed, well, ordinary—once you got past the fur and fangs and odd diet choices. It's not that she was prejudiced; she wanted to keep an open mind. Yet...

Stella was still talking up the guy's charms. "And since you can't smell, anyway, you are a perfect match. Now I will warn you, he may seem a little stiff at first, but I know you're going to find him funny and engaging—and once he warms up to you, he'll be with your forever."

Vida smirked. "'Till death do we part?"

"Darling, death is not going to keep this man from you."

She sure could use that kind of devotion. "So, is this a friend of Rolf? Is he...like Rolf?" Vida raised her eyebrows. Stella's boyfriend was a werewolf, and her stories of his prowess were bested only by the smile she wore the morning after a big date.

Stella leaned over conspiratorially. "My dear, he may be a little stiff, but he is, as they say, stiff."

"All right. Double date." Vida hated to admit it, but that decided her. It had been a long time.

That weekend, Vida got off work, dressed in her gaterskin sandals and black dress with the flirty skirt, and went to meet Stella at Out of the Dark. Stella had been trying for ages to get her to go to the 24-hour dance club; but having been raised in a small Pennsylvania town where "clubbing" was something you did to snakes in the basement, she'd grown up associating nightclubs with drugs, date rapes, and other depravities her mother would never explain. And those were the normal ones.

Even though it was ten in the morning, there were so many people on the dance floor she wasn't sure how anyone could dance. The music was loud, and the strobing lights assaulted her eyes. Still, once the shock wore off, it seemed rather ordinary.

If you discounted the fur and fangs and odd things that passed for snacks, of course.

Stella led them through the revelers toward a table in the back, stopping to hug a person here, offer her neck teasingly there. Once, she leaned over to sniff someone's behind.

Vida felt someone flip up the back of her skirt. She squealed and whirled but no one was there.

"That's Don, a poltergeist. Just ignore him, darling."

They found Rolf at the back table sitting next to a tall, dark-haired gentleman. Stella was right: from this angle at least, he was easy on the eyes. Maybe a little formal in his choice of suit, but Vida was the daughter of the Pillar of the Community of Toolittle, Pennsylvania. She could appreciate a sharp-dressed man. Still, there was something about his face she couldn't quite put her finger on.

Rolf smacked him on the shoulder and pointed. He turned to look.

Vida squeaked and grabbed her friend's arm. She hissed, "Stella! You never said he was a—" She lowered her voice further. "*A zombie.*"

Stella rolled her eyes. "Well, darling, I thought you'd have figured that out. Now make nice. You promised to keep an open mind."

"Nice. Right. Okay." She released her friend, smoothed her skirts, and prepared to open her mind. *I can make nice. It's one date. It's not like I have to...romance the dead...*

"Don't whimper, my dear. It's not attractive."

Rolf pulled Stella onto his lap, giving Vida an offhand wave by way of greeting, and the couple immediately locked lips. The man, however, stood and offered her a slight bow.

"Miss Vida Hadanoff. A pleasure to meet you. I am Mortimer Stahl. My friends call me Mort." He smiled, acknowledging the irony of his name.

Vida gave what she hoped looked like a pleasant smile. "Of course. I mean, likewise. No, wait, I—"

"—could use a drink?" he asked. He pulled out her chair for her, then took his seat and waved for the waiter.

Vida blanched when the misty form bearing a very solid drink tray floated up, but Mort just said, "We'll have a Pink Lady and a Howler for the preoccupied couple, an Intel on Ice for me, and..." He raised his eyebrows at Vida.

"Um... Iced Intel sounds interesting."

A snort emitted from the mist.

Mort smiled slowly. It didn't quite reach his eyes. Vida found it very disconcerting. "I don't think you'd find it to your taste," he said.

Again, the mist snorted.

"Oh. Then...a strawberry daiquiri. No, wait. A margarita."

"*Una margarita por la señorita mas bonita,*" Mort said.

Raspberry sounds came from the fog; then it left.

Mort shook his head. "You'll have to forgive Misty. It's hard for her to keep a job."

"Because she's a ghost?"

"Because she's so rude." Mort turned his chair slightly, so he could face her. Again, she found herself drawn to and repelled by his expressionless eyes.

"Stella tells me you work at the antiquities department at the state museum. What is it you do?"

"Well, I'm a restorer..."

Stella was right: Mort was a good listener. He was also funny and insightful. So, what if he couldn't dance—though he did a passable Robot—and she had to slow her steps to match his shambling walk as he escorted her home? When he asked to see her again, she found herself saying yes.

As one date led to another, she found they warmed to each other quite well indeed.

**

Her parents had never traveled farther than Philadelphia, and then only to escort Vida's class on a field trip to the Liberty Bell. Thus, Mort insisted that they fly up to Pennsylvania so he could meet them on their own turf. "Besides, it will be good to get out of the heat," he'd said.

He'd even gone to the Z-spa before the trip for a full exfoliation-and-deodorizing treatment with a complete fluid change. He also had his joints lubricated, something Vida especially appreciated.

She got him settled in his room at the Comfort Inn outside of Toolittle, then called her parents and met them in the lobby.

She groaned when she saw that they'd brought Jason along. She so did not need her little brother for this conversation, even if he was 37.

Couldn't be helped. She embraced them all, then led them to a table in the free continental breakfast area. The bagels and OJ were gone, but she couldn't eat now, anyway. Mort had brought his own food in an electric cooler.

She sat across them and smiled so brightly her teeth hurt. "Mom? Dad? I want to get married."

Jason snorted. "Big surprise."

Her smile soured.

"Now, dear, don't look like that," her mother told her. "I'm sure Jacey just meant he realizes you've found True Love."

"Yeah. That's it. Thanks, Ma." His smug expression belonged on an eight-year-old.

Her father cleared his throat. "So where is this man who's won the heart of my little girl?"

"He's in the room. I wanted to talk to you first. To...explain."

Jason barked a knowing laugh. Her parents just waited, eyes wide and clueless.

"Mortimer—Mort—is... life-challenged."

"Loser!" Jason translated.

"He's not! He's very responsible!"

"So, he has a good job?" her father persisted.

"Yes, Daddy! As a matter of fact, he's a night watchman at the museum."

"Yeah? You get him that job?" Jason sneered.

"You were adopted, you know!"

"Ma!"

"Well, Jacey, it's true. You're the child we chose to love." She patted his bristly cheek.

Vida strove to regain the thread of conversation. "He was working security at the morgue. He got the museum job so he could be with me more."

As she'd hoped, her mother cooed.

Jason snorted. "Probably didn't like the morgue. Who'd want to spend the night with some creepy stiff?"

Vida had the sudden urge to bite her cuticles. *I have to go on. I love him.* She squared her shoulders and tried again. "Listen, when I said, 'life-challenged...'"

"Drugs?" her father asked.

"Depraved," Jason guessed.

"Gay?" her mother whispered.

"No, no, no! He's paranormal!"

Jason rolled his eyes. "Like your friend, Stellar?"

"Stel-*la*. And Stella is psychic, not paranormal. Mort is..." She couldn't say it. They were going to hate him even before they met him. Any paranormals within a hundred miles of her hometown knew to keep their differences "under the moon." That's just how it was here.

Her mother set a hand on her trembling one. "Honey. It doesn't matter. If you love him and he loves you, that's enough for us. Right, boys?"

Her father nodded grudgingly.

Jason shrugged. "It's not like you're getting any younger. Or thinner."

"Mom!"

"Jacey! Come on, honey. Let's meet your intended."

Vida swallowed back her trepidation and stood. "Okay. Just promise you'll keep an open mind, please?"

***

A few minutes later, Vida was in the hotel bathroom, running a washcloth under cold water to revive her mother. Mort stood behind her.

"You didn't tell them, did you?"

"I tried. I really did. We should just go."

He set his hands on her shoulders. "It's all right. They're your family. That's important. Don't worry. We'll get through this."

Vida nodded and hurried back to set the washcloth on her mother's forehead.

"Good one, Sis," Jason sneered, casting a dark look at her intended.

Her mother moaned and blinked. Then she turned her head toward the pillow and sat up with a start. "I'm in its bed!"

"On," Mort replied, ignoring the insulting pronoun. "And it's the hotel's bed. I've not touched it yet."

Nonetheless, she rose and started for the chair. Her husband cleared his throat and shook his head slightly, glancing from it to Mort. She sat back down on the bed. Vida took the rejected seat, Mort standing behind her, a hand on the chair back.

He spoke. "Mr. and Mrs. Hadanoff. Jason. Perhaps if I explain a little about my condition?"

"I'm not ignorant, Mr. Stahl," her father said. "I know all about the genetic experiments and mutating DNA against God's plan. You're an abomination."

"Daddy!"

"Not an abomination, sir. An accident, perhaps? Providence, maybe. My grandmother was given treatments to extend her life during her pregnancy; my mother inherited the changed gene, as did I."

"And you want to pass this curse to my grandchildren?"

"Kids?" Jason exclaimed. "That means you'd have to—ugh! That's so gross, and I mean for the both of you!"

Her father grumbled, "Have you any idea how people of this community will talk if our daughter…"

Her mother raised pleading hands. "Vida, dear, do you understand the dangers of wild living now? Please, honey, just come home!"

"Stop it!" Vida stood. "Just stop it! You don't understand anything. I knew how you'd react. I wanted to elope, but Mort wanted to come here, and why? So he could ask for your blessings! Because he knows I love you and he loves me and he's an honorable and good man and I don't care if he's undead. I love him!"

She burst into tears.

Mortimer put his arms around her, but her father grabbed her to pull her toward him.

"Away from her. What possible comfort can you provide?"

Jason snorted. "Cold."

"Shut up!" Vida sobbed.

Suddenly her mother stood and wrapped her arms around both Vida and Mort. She turned her head toward her husband and son.

"That is enough, both of you! Vida has made her choice, and if they love each other, that's good enough for me—for all of us. We're Hadanoffs. Pillars of the Community. We can do anything!"

***

"I'm sorry, Mom. I can't do this." Vida sighed, torn between crying and raging. Three weeks before the wedding, and things just seemed to be falling apart! It wasn't fair.

Her mother put an arm around her shoulder and caressed her hair. "Shh, honey. It's all right. I'm sure he understands."

The wedding planner slid back the menu to Gordo, the caterer, and glared at him expectantly.

Gordo huffed. "And what is wrong with it this time?"

Vida gritted her teeth and leaned across the table. "The same thing that's been wrong the last four. Listen, the Lugosis are flying—flying—" She made flapping motions with her hands. "—halfway across the country for this wedding, and I will not insult them by serving a meal with garlic."

"And let's not forget the Lupos," her mother added. "You put beef back in the menu. We told you what that does to those of the werewolf persuasion."

Gordo threw his hands in the air, and the planner said, "Surely if we offer some choices...?"

"No! Open bar will be bad enough with some of Jason's friends. I'm not adding a bunch of red-meat intoxicated *dogmen*!"

"Vida!"

"Sorry, Mom. I'm just... I'm sorry." She pressed her fingers against her eyes.

Gordo's stubborn expression gentled. He reached into his briefcase and pulled out a large binder and pushed it towards her. "What do you suggest I cook that does not involve beef or garlic? But if you say cold cuts, you may take that up with the Giant."

Actually, ordering from the grocery store was sounding pretty good to Vida, but that would hardly do for a Pillar of the Community like the Hadanoff family.

Now her mother looked ready to reach for the tissues herself, so she grabbed the binder and started flipping through it. "How about Indian? Aren't there a lot of Hindu and Buddhist dishes..."

"Oh, honey," her mother protested. "I don't know." She lowered her voice. "That's so pagan."

"*Vegan*, Mom, and there are chicken dishes, too."

However, the planner and the caterer, relieved to see Vida happy with some choice, jumped in.

"I can do Tandoori Chicken. Or Tandoori Quail! Very classy."

"I've had an inspiration!" the planner declared with a theatric wave of her arms. "I've been racking my brains over what to do for the reception theme. What about A Night in Bollywood?"

"I don't know," her mother hedged, but she didn't faint. She had come a long way in the last six months. Very little gave her 'the vapors' any longer.

"Mom, that sounds kind of fun. Maybe we could teach the wedding party a dance?"

"Mrs. Hadanoff, this will be the wedding of the decade. Why not have a reception they will remember? Trust me; we'll make it tasteful and fun. I'm already seeing the room lined with tasseled fabrics in turquoise and orange. I wonder if I can find a small elephant?"

"Well, if it will satisfy everyone..." her mother hedged, then looked at Vida.

Vida frowned. "Quail? All right, but we'll need to pre-slice it. I think there might be some latent Labrador impulses..."

Gordo sighed and slumped in his chair. "Whatever you wish."

***

Stella rushed into the bride's room, a flurry of orange scarves and turquoise chiffon.

"Everything's almost ready, Darling. The guests are all seated quietly now."

"Did Minister Greatlove put away his cross?" Vida asked worriedly. She held one hand to her chin while her bridesmaids fussed with her veil.

Greatlove, their family minister, had refused to conduct the ceremony, but fortunately, one of the pastors from Mort's church had agreed to fly up for the day. However, the local minister knew better than to insult the Pillars of the Community by not attending the wedding of the decade—and he'd thought it a chance to do a little ol' fashioned exorcising while he was at it.

"No, darling, but he's just caressing it and muttering, not trying to shove it in people's faces now. I think Bella gushing over how lovely it was gave him pause."

"Well, then, there's only one crisis left." Vida removed her hand.

The ladies screamed as one.

"Zit!"

The room exploded into a flurry of bridesmaids reaching for purses, pulling out exfoliants and creams, and comparing make-up bases. Vida stared at the mirror, sure the offending pimple was growing bigger as she watched. She fought back hard against whimpers.

"Ladies!" Stella clapped her hands and they stilled. "We do not panic before the wedding. It is not attractive. There is a simple and elegant solution. Now remain calm and wait for my return."

She fluttered out the door.

As soon as it shut behind the last bit of scarf, her childhood friend Ellen asked, "Are you sure you want to go through with this?"

Vida was staring at the mirror, fighting the urge to pop. "Oh, if Stella says she has a solution—"

"No, I mean marrying. Him. Isn't that, like, necrophilia or something?"

"Oh, honestly!" Trillian, her other friend since elementary school, scoffed. Ever since Vida had announced the engagement, Trillie had been sending her clippings of articles about zombies that she'd found in magazines from *National Geographic* to *Cosmo* to *Life*. "They aren't dead. They're *un*-dead. It's a big difference, you know. But what I want to know is: Is it true what they say? You know—about zombie men being 'stiff'?"

"I don't kiss and tell," Vida declared haughtily, then treated them to one of Stella's Patented Satisfied Smiles.

Again, the room erupted into screams.

"Honestly, darlings," Stella said as she fluttered back into the room. "I told you there was no need for alarm. Now someone find me a Q-Tip. Thank you. Hold still, darling." She dabbed something herbal and cool on Vida's chin.

A tense moment as five sets of eyes watched Vida's face. Then: "Oooooooo!"

"Is it gone?" Vida exclaimed.

"It is calmer than you, and it will have faded before you can say, 'I do.'"

Vida looked at the mirror and gave a happy cry. "What is that stuff?"

"Brazilian embalming fluid."

This time Vida joined her bridesmaids in screaming, but Trillian said, "Where can I get some of that?"

***

The Master of Ceremonies for the reception tapped the mic and spoke in his best Vegas Lounge Lizard voice. "Ladies and Gentlemen—"

"Sires and bitches!" Jason hollered out. Vida's mom gasped, but the werewolves howled their approval while others laughed.

The DJ pointed at Jason with a wink. "Whatever you all call yourselves and whatever you want others to call you—on behalf of the Hadanoff and the Stahl families, I'd like to welcome you to the reception of the decade!"

Applause, and the spotlight turned to Vida and Mort. Vida leaned against her husband's shoulder, happier than she'd ever been in her life.

"I'd like to invite the...lively couple—" The drummer did a rim shot and the audience supplied groans and catcalls, which the MC ignored. "—to the dance floor for their first dance as husband and wife."

Mort had grudgingly agreed to try a Bollywood group dance, but only after he'd had his slow dance with his bride. As the band started up with an instrumental version of "Every Breath You Take," Vida slipped into

Mort's arms, and they shuffled along the dance floor.

"You're dancing very well," she murmured, trying not to act surprised.

"Your mother gave me lessons, and I tried a new fluid at the spa—Brazilian."

Vida leaned back. "My zit!"

"Stella said you were distraught. You know that it would not have made a difference to me. You'll always be beautiful."

Vida sighed and leaned into his shoulder. After a few minutes, others joined the dance.

People left their tables and started to mingle. Bella and Minister Greatlove were deep in some theological debate. Vida saw her cousin escort Misty to the floor. He didn't seem to know where to put his hands. Meanwhile in a corner behind the elephant stall...

"Mort!" Vida hissed. "Is that my brother and Rolf's sister?"

He turned slightly. "You didn't notice how friendly he and Hurra had gotten at the rehearsal dinner?"

"They're tongue-kissing! That is so gross—for her, I mean."

"Now, Vida. You don't know where else her tongue has been."

"You can say the same for his."

Mort chuckled, a deep rumbling in his chest. When they'd first met, his laugh had sounded asthmatic and forced; she'd had to teach him over the year. She leaned back against him, listening and sighing with contentment.

"You know," he said. "He approached me after the dinner."

"Oh, no! What did he say?"

"I think the exact words were, 'You hurt my sister and I will slice you into small parts and feed you to the fishes. Let's see you undie from that.'"

"Really? That's so adorable! I didn't think he cared."

"Of course, he does. He just has an odd way of showing it."

Vida watched as her mom marched behind the elephant stall and came out dragging her brother by the ear while Hurra followed, adjusting her skirts and smiling smugly. "Think he's met his match?" she asked.

"Perhaps. I do know one thing for certain, however. I have met my match in you."

"You'd better have, since we're married now—'Till death do we part."

"Death can't keep me from you," he said and smiled his slow smile.

Vida gazed into his eyes. Once, she'd thought them devoid of emotion; dead, as he was.

Now she knew so much better.

Recipe for Intel on Ice

1/2 oz amaretto almond liqueur
1/2 oz Southern Comfort® peach liqueur
1 oz puréed brains

ABOUT THE AUTHORS

About Colleen Drippé

Colleen Drippé writes science fiction novels and a multitude of stories of science fiction, fantasy, and horror for various small press magazines and anthologies. When not writing genre fiction, Mrs. Drippé writes for a children's magazine and has also published articles on raising children, essays on this and that, Christmas stories and four children's books. She is a grandmother seventeen times over (and probably more to come) and lives with her husband, cats, and books. Her husband, Paul, is an artist. Learn more at https://colleendrippe.com/

About Karina Fabian

By day, Karina writes product reviews and marketing content, but after hours, she's a snarky dragon who thinks he saves the world all-too regularly, a crew of redneck space explorers, a zombie exterminator who just wants her world clear of undead vermin, and Catholic religious sisters whose callings have taken them off our world. When she's not converting her wild tales to stories, she's enjoying Florida life with her husband, Rob. They have four adult children, two dogs, and a rocket company. Find all her books at http://karinafabian.com.